20th April 2023

## Somewhere in Wales

I am again sitting at the old arts and crafts bureau which was left to me indirectly by my aunt. It is a lovely sunny day an I have the French doors open onto the deck at the back of the house on which Murph the dog is sunning herself.

The Outlander world has turned slightly since my last publication, series seven part one will air on 16th June 2023 so we are told, part two will air in 2024 and yes there will be an eighth and final series of the TV show. Diana meanwhile is forging her way through Book Ten., and now the burning questions are:

What will the ending be?

Where will the series end in comparison to the books?

What is the secret of Jamie's ghost?

I do not have the answers to any of those questions.

Since my last effort 'Facing the Storm' I have continued to publish a poem a day on social media for your enjoyment. It has become the coffee time poem and a bit of an institution. I have also published two volumes of what is essentially a 'chronological complete works series called Mille Basia, I hope to publish volume three in the near future.

I have also been working on a novel, yes its historical, yes it's a bit of a romance but it is also a murder mystery. It is based in Wales where else!

The poems published in Between the Lines have all been written since then and many will not have been seen before.

Again, I will stress that what I write is a tribute and inspired by the books of Diana Gabaldon and also the Starz TV Series.

My cover artwork is again a pastel work by Lyn Fuller, who I cannot thank enough for her kindness in allowing me to use her work to enhance mine.

All proceeds from the sale of my work are donated to Riding for the Disabled, a charity which provides therapy for a wide range of conditions through the medium of horses. It is a charity close to my heart from which I have personally benefitted and with which I volunteer as a riding coach in training.

Without further ado

Put the kettle on or make a drink of your choice and most of all enjoy.

Contents

# Reading Between the Lines

## The last one

Is there no end to all the blood,
Is there no end to war
The endless line of wounded
Streaming through the door.

Bare hands staunch the bleeding,
Ears immune to screams,
Pain wracked bodies lie and wait
They all invade my dreams,

Boys fresh from the country,
Boys not even men,
Full of hope, and full of fear
Sent to this devils den.

The blood that stains my apron,
The guts that stain my hands
Yet another young life lost
For freedom in these lands.

Forceps please, retractor now
I bark instructions, plain
Do not let him see the wound
Morphine for the pain

With all my heart I pray he lives
For he is the last,
The guns have ceased their endless fire
At last, this war is passed.

Eyes closed in resignation
No more I can do,
He must not know his epitaph
The last one in my queue.

Pass the bottle, raise it high,
To those who went before
To peace, to life, to all we lost
And to the end of war.,

To the faces I will see in dreams
That call me from their grave
To the ones who lie cold in the ground
The ones we could not save.

## Going for a Waulk

Sitting round a table,
Ladies gathered for a drink,
My mug is full of cider,
I'm enjoying this, I think.

Why, this is not a social
We are here to work,
Hard on the hands is waulking wool,
And no time now tae shirk,

Singing songs with rhythm,
Whose words go back in time,
Keep the beat and work the cloth,
There's method in the rhyme.

More cider Claire, the jug is poured,
If I am not deceived,
It's Strong and diuretic,
Should I be relieved?

Push and pull the bolt of cloth,
Work the warp and weft,
I need to find the privy soon!
It's really time I left.

The song has stopped, the ladies laugh!
To them there's naught amiss,
There's a bucket in the corner,
In which to take a piss.

I raise my skirts for action,
Squat and take my aim,
That pungent smell, just like the wool
It really is the same,

Ladies please don't tell me,
The use for what I've quaffed,
You soak the cloth in urine?
Aye, it helps tae mak it soft,

And tis an opportunity,
For us tae sit and talk,
We tell our menfolk only
That we're going fer a waulk!

## Not a witch

For miles we rode in silence
The horses breath came fast
Safety found in distance
Solace found at last.

The forest our companion
The hills our loyal friends
The mountains were our hiding place
Was here we'd make amends.

When at last he deigned to talk
The voice that broke the silence
Was strained with hoarse emotion
Taut with reined in violence

Once again he risked his life
Once more he had saved mine
What answers would he want from me
What lies would I design.

Tell me what and who you are,
Your face betrays your lies
Some things I have a right to know
Are hid behind your eyes

And so, I told him everything,
I hoped he would believe
Forgive me for my treachery,
Then would he let me leave.

He led me to that ring of stones
Soft kisses seared my face
His imprint left forever
In one final embrace.

As I watched him turn and walk
His shoulders slumped I thought,
I added up the things I missed,
The sum of it was nought.

I sat and packed a life away,
Regret would be a crime,
My old life in the future lost
To stay here in his time.

I found him lying restless
Sorrow creased his brow.
Wake up soldier take me home,
I'm yours forever now.

## Last Request

I din'nae ask this lightly,
I can nae take much more,
My body mends despite it all,
My mind has seen hells door.

Ye would nae keep a dog alive
Ye'd ease it from its pain,
I beg ye do not let her in
She can nae cure my brain.

I cannot voice the way I feel,
I will not have her see
The vilest, filthy, depraved acts
That man performed on me

If ye had nae found me
I would have met the rope,
Happy just to be at peace,
Accept I have no hope.

Get yer heid out o' the parritch man,
Ye dinna think of Claire,
If Ye'd make her a widow,
I will na let ye, Ken?

Let her weave her magic man,
Allow her soul back in,
Din'nae think of leavin' her,
She'll no forgive that sin!

I conjured up his demons,
He fought me to the floor
Tooth and nail, we grappled,
All sense went through the door,

Then at last exhausted
In body and in mind,
Our tears lay mixed on sweat soaked skin,
And peace at last he'd find

## Pretty Britches

Gilded French formality,
Versailles at her best,
The finest of French fashion,
The King disposed to jest!

Madame your speech is perfect,
You grace us with your style,
Le Roi applauds your radiance,
You light us with your smile,

And who is this, this Englishman,
A soldier of the Crown,
With the manners of a peasant,
His accent makes us frown,

Maybe I should make him kneel
If favours he must ask,
So serious his countenance,
Well hid behind a mask.

You English are so literal,
Can you not see I tease
Do not spoil such pretty britches.
Captain get up from your knees

## No Death Today

I watched my life go safely
Through a granite ring of stone.
Returning to Drummossie moor
To face my fate alone

British cannon pounded
It's blast the blast that stuns
Call the charge! Don't let us stand
Like fodder for the guns

Volley fire came on in sheets
Aimed below our knees
Cut the front rank down in droves
Then kill us as they please.

Barefoot now I did not care
Blood crazed if you will
I found myself behind their guns
My broadsword had its fill.

How many lives I took that day
Memory calls me liar!
Slaughtered Clansmen all around
Waiting for the pyre.

All night I lay beneath his corpse
Eyes sealed tight with blood
As Black Jack Randall breathed his last
And pinned me in the mud.

I saw you through the freezing rain
I called across the time
The silence of the dead rang out
For men killed in their prime.

Dragged from the field, with mortal wounds
They will na let me lie
I listened as he took the names
Of Those about to die.

A soldiers death, a musket ball
But mine is not to be,
Again, saved by a Redcoat
Am I never to be free!

# Lost in fog

My face was red from tooth sore gums.
My temper fit to burst,
I kicked and screamed and threw things,
Would not stay with my nurse.

You took me from the playroom,
Best you take me back,
No, I'm not going anywhere!
If I cannot ride with Mac!

A fine day for a picnic,
It's peaceful on the fell,
The yowling of his lordship,
Well, that should break the spell!

My clothes are tight and itchy,
They are not fitting right,
A toddler in a corset,
Are you surprised I bite.

Mama is scolding Betty.
She's in trouble I suppose.
Oh, look there is a beetle,
It fits right up my nose.

I'm tired now and grumpy,
No one wants to play,
I could hide between those stones,
Unseen I crawl away,

I lay there on the hillside,
Curled up like a dog,
Then the world went damp and grey,
All around was fog.

Mac! Please help, I need you,
I'm cold and so afraid,
Mac! Please come and find me.
I'm sorry that I strayed.

William, where are you?
My lungs were fit to burst,
William, stay where you are,
Where has he gone, I cursed!

My mind descends tae panic,
I'm worrit tae ma bones!
Was it a father's instinct?
Made me look between those stones,

I picked ye up and held ye,
Comforted yer cries,
Best yer granny does'nae see.
The tears form in my eyes.

I held ye close inside my arms,
It made my body shake,
To feel a bond between us forge,
That I will never break!

## Hay and Molasses

Ye'd nagged and screamed and tantrum'd
Ye always got yer way,
They brought ye tae the stables,
Tae bide there fer the day,

A little lad in britches,
Barely out of clouts,
Brought tae see the horses.
Ye turned ma world about.

I taught ye all the horses names,
Then we made the mash,
I told ye NO, ye listened,
With out a great strammash,

Ye played with hay and harness,
Ye helped me with the feed,
Sticky with molasses,
Ye made a mess indeed,

Riding on my shoulders,
That day ye had such fun,
My heart leapt when a farmer.
Mistook ye fer ma son.

I'd treasure every moment.
That time ye spent with me.
Wishing I could keep ye there.
But that could never be,

Remembered too another bairn.
Lost in another time,
Pray them safe, she and the child,
That can'nae be a crime.

The stable clock is chiming,
It says 'tis half past three,
Best I take ye to the house,
Time for yer lordship's tea!

## Separate Bunks

I will na have ye sharing,
She is'nae yet yer wife,
Handfast does nae cut it,
Her mother will cause strife

There is nae point in begging,
And din nae think I'm blind
Fergus ye will share with me,
I will nae change ma mind.

Marsali shall sleep with Claire,
Until we find a priest,
Ye will have vows, if not in church,
Ye will do that at least.

Canoodling in corners,
Love amidst the ropes,
No privacy is found at sea,
So don't build up your hopes,

My cabin mate thinks me a witch,
Or at the best a whore,
At least I have the biggest berth,
I hope she doesn't snore.

Fergus is frustrated,
Marsali hates his guts,
Sleeping without Jamie
The lack will drive me nuts.

Sassenach, contain yer lust,
I've aching in my crotch,
I'll meet ye on the afterdeck,
When they change the watch.

## Fine Dining

Invited out to dinner,
Dining in fine style,
A chance sell an asset,
And network for a while,

I'm sitting at a table,
Am I mutton dressed as lamb,
Finest wares out on display,
Please pass another clam!

Men in conversation
Take a closer look,
The ruby hanging round my neck,
Really was the hook.

Dangled in no setting
Except the wearers skin,
This flawless stone was guaranteed
To draw a buyer in.

The sale negotiated,
We've gold then in our purse,
Will we find our destiny,
Or suffer something worse

# An Offer. can I refuse?

I've an offer Mr Fraser,
The land needs such as you,
Men to colonise this land,
Men to keep order too

Land where you could prosper,
Ye know I know your aunt,
Fertile land a plenty,
And the power of grant.

Governor I have read the law,
I really do not see,
How the Kings conditions
Can apply to me.

Male and white and Protestant
Thirty years of age,
This is written down as law,
I've seen it on the page.

I can'nae take yer offer,
I will nae find a spot.
I'm Male and white and of that age
But Protestant I am not!

Sit and take a brandy,
Tryon poured the large,
The offers there, negotiate
Before you catch the barge.

Northern Carolina
Needs the like of you
Unafraid to take a risk,
Or stretch a law or two.

Would be a shame to turn it down,
The acreage is great,
Ten thousand in the back lands,
You'd have plenty on your plate.

We are far from London,
You are troubling no one
And you see there is the Law
And then there's what is done.

## A hand of cards

Privacy so nearly gained,
The moments passion shattered,
Heat dispersed, in words so cool,
One wouldn't think I mattered!

Saving face and dignity,
I think I catch the gist,
He's just deferred a night with me,
For a hand of whist.

A game of skill and luck at cards,
For those who have a stake,
He'd take the last gold thing I own
Franks ring, for goodness sake!

Well, let him have the two of them,
Both marks of possession,
Bloody man, he'd gamble both,
To vent his damned aggression,

He wagers with part of my life,
That stake part of my soul,
He has some other purpose,
To hurt me, not his goal.

He'll ride his luck, right to the edge,
Oblivious of course,
My feelings trampled in the dirt,
And under Wylie's horse!

That night I dreamed of Friesians,
Black stallions in the night,
Then the king of Ireland,
Woke me up in fright.

A hand beneath the bedclothes,
Is massaging my toe,
Curling round my instep,
It's grip not letting go.

Wandering hand in darkness,
Large and deft of touch,
Assured of destination,
The release I crave so much.

Its owner hid in shadows,
I pray my thoughts are right,
The hand that comes to claim me
Is my Scotsman of the night.

Morning comes, dishevelled,
Hungover, dressed in haste,
Waiting in the doorway
All trace of guilt erased

A hand of cards, a fist of rings,
Did I doubt he'd win,
An eyebrow raised, a laser stare,
Just a hint of grin.

Gold for left, silver right,
Reclaimed in the stable,
As horses wake and humans stir,
We'll stand up if we're able.

# Brave Wee Thing

I'd thought tae be so gentle,
Bring her back to peace,
Soothe her body and her mind,
But her demons I release,

Wine tae blur the memories,
Wine tae dim the light,
Wine will draw her from her shell
wine will make her fight,

Blood-stained lips and raking teeth,
Clawing, raking nails,
Urge me to a darker place
A place where reason fails,

Sweat soaked muscles strained in need,
Scent of untamed lust,
Locked together, fused as one
We grind ourselves to dust,

Brave wee thing, I feel you rise,
Your spirit fights with mine,
You are here, you are whole
Now live, not just survive.

My silent tears will mix with yours
As your demons watch you weep,
This sobbing wretch will cry with you,
Even as we sleep.

## Christmas Surprise

Wool supplied by Jenny's sheep,
Spun by Marsalis's hand,
On the wheel made by Brianna,
Dyed as Lizzie planned,

Balls of yarn in many hues,
The colours of the trees,
Kept me busy through the nights,
A secret e'en from bees.

I'm not the best at klickit,
Young Ian taught me best,
Easy for a Scotsman,
They learn it at the breast!

My needles are best stitching,
Mending holes in skin,
I'm like a pig with chopsticks!
But I am not giving in.

Sticking to the pattern
That was with danger fraught,
Well, it was in Gaelic,
So, I read it as I thought.

Proud as punch I finished,
My homemade Christmas gift,
Crept up to the bedroom
Dressed only in my shift,

My effort lies beneath the tree,
Completed before dawn,
Something special for himself,
A surprise for Christmas morn.

What are these now Sassenach?,
He held them up with pride,
The tears of mirth that followed
Would not be denied,

One was long and baggy,
Striped like candy cane,
The other much much smaller,
How could I explain!

Sassenach, they're wonderful,
He gasped between guffaws,
Put a wee flap at the back,
They could be winter drawers!

I ken they're meant as stockings,
I din'nae mean tae laugh
Sure, one can keep my cock warm,
The other is a scarf!

Back upstairs now Sassenach,
I mean tae wear ma gift,
I can'nae wait tae get ma Christmas sock
Right Under yer shift!

## Happy New Year

Open all the widows
Open all the doors,
Time to let the old year out,
Time to take a pause,

Raise a glass and make a toast,
This last year is no more,
Drink a dram and see her off,
A strange one to be sure.

Remember though the good times,
There will have been a few,
Every year holds memories,
Move on without ado.

Life is for the living,
Do not be downcast.
Nothing is there to be gained,
From living in the past.

Throw open all your windows,
Open up your doors,
Welcome in a fresh new year,
And start a dream that's yours.

## Dr Rawlins Casebook

Dr Rawlins casebook
Drew me back a page,
His journey out to River Run,
A man must earn a wage.

A journey fraught with danger,
Through rain and hail and mud
The patient Aunt Jocasta.
She of Jamie's blood.

Detailed diagnosis,
Noted here to see,
But what is all this Latin,
It reads like Greek to me.

He's also treating Hector,
cystitis I am sure,
Pain on micturition,
Cranberry juice the cure!

Laudanum for sleeping,
That's parr for the course
Hector can't be sleepwalking
That dose should stop a horse!

We ponder on each meaning
Intrigue and medicine fused,
A reference French, and also Gold,
Masonic symbols used.

Who is roaming River Run,
In the dark of night,
What happened to the Doctor,
Did he die of fright.

He surely was a mason,
And saw things that he feared,
He wrote them in his casebook,
And then, he disappeared.

## Myrtle Berries

Two buckets and a picnic,
Equipment for the day,
Loaded in a goat cart,
The goat refused to play,

Foraging for berries
Just to pass the time,
Don't worry for our menfolk,
That would be a crime

An ancient flintlock pistol,
We must beware of snakes,
What else hides in the bushes
Let's go for goodness sakes,

Soft footsteps in the Myrtle,
A voice smooth as a sonnet,
Smuggler, pirate, robber,
Rapist, Stephen Bonnet.

Someone shoot him, do it now!
A knife held to my throat,
If I must die, he shall not take
My kin back to his boat.

Children run, Jemmy hide,
The pistol leaves his waist
The flintlock fires, chaos reigns
All sense of calm erased.

Not your son! Her voice is clear,
Her steps soft on the sand,
Stephen is your powder dry,
His pistol in her hand.

Brianna takes a careful aim,
his Irish bluff she calls,
His weapon primed, her aim is good,
Bonnets has no balls

## Sorcha

Sorcha, Claire, you are my light
Illuminate my days,
Without you there is nothing
All in darkness stays.

You are my dawn, you are my dusk
My winter and my spring,
You give my world a purpose,
You are it's everything.

When bleak stones held me captive
The sun would rise each day,
Each morning I was thankful
I did'na let ye stay.

I'd watch the world about her work,
Feel what love had cost,
Hidden from me by a veil,
Gone but never lost.

She goes about her business,
Revolving through the years,
If we lose hope, all we have left,
Is bitterness and tears

For you are all around me,
I thank the Lord for that
I hear ye cursing to yerself,
And talking tae the cat,

And here ye are all skin and bone,
And I a worn-out wretch,
Still Ye'd take me to yer bed,
Oh, flesh of ma flesh

Din'nae leave me Sassenach
I'd be angry should ye die,
For then all hope has left my world,
Without good reason aye.

# Enough

We've never had much place for 'things'
We've led a migrant life,
Home is where we lay our heads,
Or where I find my wife,

All the things we've left behind,
No matter what they cost,
She never seems to miss them,
She just accepts their loss.

If we could nae carry it,
If it was nae gold
Sentiment would play no part,
Everything was sold

Now we have some respite,
For now, the fight has ceased
A quiet space between the wars,
A little spot of peace.

A set of pearls, a silver ring,
All she has of me,
What then should I leave for her,
Underneath the tree.

A moments peace and quiet,
A lifetime in my arms,
My body and immortal soul
To keep her safe from harm

Devotion, yes and passion
Until we turn to dust,
Faithfulness and honesty
And just a hint of lust.

I'd love tae see her dressed in silks,
More often she's in rags,
Leather apron round her waist,
Brandishing my dags.

She's no' materialistic,
She has nae need for 'stuff'
I'll just be me, under the tree,
And pray that is enough.

# Dreamscape

I dreamed I saw ye Sassenach,
Ye sat there framed in light,
I did'na ken how old ye were,
Yer hair, it was' nae white.

I felt that Ye'd been writing
Ye had that studious look,
The one ye get when things ye've done
ye write them in yer book

I can nae say twas in yer past,
My dreams go where they will,
I could dream tartan flutterbys,
But they will no' keep still.

Do I dream our future then
See things that will be,
Should I die, then you must go
You, the bairns, and Bree.

Ye ken I can nae keep ye safe,
If all around is war,
Promise me that you at least
Will step back through times door.

One last stone, tis all we have
One stone can take ye back,
Tis the colour of the future aye,
One stone, a diamond, black.

Why would I go, when all is here,
My life is built with you,
This family, this time, this life
I'd stay and see things through.

There's nothing now beyond those stones,
I've sacrificed my time,
Don't think you can be shot of me
Because I'm past my prime.

He placed that diamond in my hand,
He begged me not to stay,
I'd rather die than leave him
I threw the stone away

Together we will ride the storm,
And if we can survive,
Home is here and in this time
And for now, we are alive

And if you have that dream again
You aggravating Scot
Please tell me if the butterflies,
Have tartan wings or not.

## Dear Jamie

Dear Jamie,
Since I've known you,
You've had scant care for rule
In God's name do not do this
Tis the action of a fool.

Stubborn and intemperate
Tell me that you're not,
Honourable and intelligent,
Foolhardy, reckless, Scot!

Named again a traitor,
A known seditionist.
Denounce these rumours Jamie please
They have you on their list.

Your family endangered,
Don't play fast and loose,
The only end that I can see
Is your neck in a noose.

The Crown will send its army,
Your cause will be suppressed,
The King will have his justice,
You surely face arrest,

For sake of ties between us
And history long gone.
Reaffirm your loyalty,
Yours in friendship - John

Dear John,

I fear your letter comes too late,
my course is set tis plain,
I'd not put you in danger,
I shall not write again!

I sever ties between us,
With the greatest of regret,
Your humblest Jamie Fraser,
P.S. They have nae caught me yet!

## Meeting on the Dock

Disembarking soldiers
Chaos on the dock,
Another day in Wilmington,
An unexpected shock.

Brianna on a mission,
Is mercy in her head
Or is her purpose really
To make sure Bonnets dead.

Who is that with Lord John Grey,
He surely looks like Da,
But Da dressed as a redcoat,
Too far-fetched by far.

He has his height, He has his grace
Lord John what a surprise,
Who is this copy of my father,
Damn, he even has his eyes.

His Lordship, consternated
Flapping like the birds
Seeing my mental penny drop,
Explains his loss of words.

Helwater, seventeen fifty-eight!
And yes your mother knows,
He must not see your father,
My suspicion grows.

Yes you have a brother,
Please don't let him see
He can't know he's a bastard,
Do this thing for me Bree.

And so, I met my brother,
Greeted him as friend,
Knowing sure as eggs are eggs
He'll find out in the end.

# A Dance of Swords

An omen for the outcome,
Who will win the day
Predict the course of battle,
Before you meet the fray

A dance of strength and energy
Of nimble feet and grace,
Mind focused on the coming fight,
The enemy you face.

Blades a cross upon the floor,
The dancer must show skill,
Footwork swift, balance kept,
Unseen the foe you kill.

With Head bowed deep recalling
He stepped onto the floor,
Standing in a far-off land,
Beneath his feet a moor.

The formal bow, his fighting arm
Makes a courtly sweep
Sure, footed as a highland stag
My dancer starts to leap,

Back to a land of memories,
I see them in his face,
A distant sadness haunts his eyes,
Lost in time and place.

Clapping hands and stamping feet,
Mac Dubh, Mac Dubh, they roar!
He dances for the Ardsmuir men,
To appease the gods of war!

Mac Dubh will dance for all tonight,
A New Year we will meet,
When all will need to hear the call
And march to just one beat.

He sees the times a changing,
Will turn to face what comes,
Stepping lively to the music,
And dancing to wars drums

# Freedom Fighters

Why this quest for freedom,
A life lived without chains,
Why do we fight and fight again,
Til only hope remains,

The right to hold opposing views,
To worship as ye choose,
The right to raise yer children,
To walk proud in your shoes.

For honest work, of honest men
For laws that serve the weak,
Not for those self-serving,
Who for their own ends seek.

Those who take the burden,
Who shoulder all the need,
Eventually will fail the task,
Consumed by endless greed.

Will we keep moving onwards,
Drift from land to land,
Or is this place our final home,
The place we make a stand.

Where all are governed fairly,
Where no man is a slave,
Where all folk shall live safely
From cradle to the grave.

It will nae be utopia,
Tis not the way of man,
For some will always find a way,
To work around the plan.

What is the future Sassenach,
Is it with the fight,
Before I take up arms again,
Do we do what's right?

What is this dream ye talk of,
The home of brave and free,
The home of generations yet,
Will it be home for me.

We've travelled far, we've laboured hard,
We've walked between the fires,
Schemed and plotted with the best,
Honour lost and liars.

We fight on for a future,
We fight on for our kin,
For generations not yet born,
We cannot now give in.

If what you say is coming,
Will build a better place,
Tis worth the fight, to rid it
Of the worst parts of this race.

The fight goes on forever,
Somewhere always a slave,
Our eternal freedom Lass
Will come after the grave.

## Game Pie

Home is the hunter from the hill,
Quite proud of what he's shot
He bounds into my kitchen
To fill the cooking pot.

I'll have them skinned in no time,
He holds me with his eye,
How are ye wi' pastry,
I'm fancying some pie!

Hanging there below his belt,
Strung up by their tails,
A brace of plump young rabbits,
They're stew if all else fails,

Its hanging by his sporran,
Clothed in bright red hair,
Bright of eye and bushy tailed,
Can ye cook this one Claire?

Not turning from the table,
I meet his words, unphased,
'What I can do with that dead thing,
You could be quite amazed.

Now get out of the kitchen,
I need to make some stock,
I sense you are behind me
And you are playing with your cock.

Now Sassenach ye have me wrong,
Game pie is what I planned,
Ye need tae wear yer glasses
Tis a squirrel in ma hand!

# Christmas in Quebec

Christmas time away from home,
I'm stranded in Quebec,
A Convent of Ursuline Nuns
And snow up to my neck.

Did you see the northern lights,
When you were here papa,
The sky is cleared, and bright with stars,
I wonder how you are.

The sisters bid me go to mass
I'd rather watch the sky,
The glow of the aurora
Is pleasing to the eye.

The city bells are more than close
I hear them sound just fine,
I'm writing as my ears ring
It's a quarter after nine.

I write this night of warfare,
Of skirmishes and ships,
Of nuns so shocked by highlanders
With kilts hung from their hips.

I hear the sound of singing,
Candles flicker bright,
Wrapped in cloaks of darkness,
Nuns are pieces of the night.

Midnight was approaching,
I did go down to mass,
How could I miss a Christmas morn,
I'd not let this one pass,

I prayed there for Geneva
Mother of my blood
And for mama Isobel
It felt right that I should.

I wish you joy of Christmas,
Enjoy your roasted goose,
I should write more often,
There's really no excuse.

All my love to Family
And to you of course
And to my darling Dottie,
My feisty tour de force.

William Ransom signing off
The bell has just tolled two,
Borealis fills the sky,
In lights which are now blue

# A Disturbance in the ranks
### Scotland 1980's

Position free, end of the month,
I should be making merry,
What's that you say, I've got the job!
We need a secretary!

Plant inspector was the role,
I'm qualified in spades,
Are there other applicants?
I try not to sound dismayed

It's just ye are – a woman,
It's not a woman's place
Ye'd have to work with men ye see,
Ye'd not have their good grace.

A voice honed with an edge of steel,
Inherited from one
Who will not take the answer no
Who likes a battle won.

Tell me what the job entails,
What part I could not do,
Which part requires a penis,
Pray tell me, walk me through!

The only use that I can see,
Is if ye have a leak,
A man could stick it in the hole,
And stand there for a week!

There is really not a problem,
I've worked with men before,
And I've dealt with danger,
I can do the job, and more.

And so, I was appointed,
Inspector for the dam,
Look out lads, I'm on my way,
Best you call me ma'am

A woman should' na be the boss,
It is nae right ye ken,
Does she think she rules us?
She'll have her comeuppance then.

Kissed without consent

Loving without knowing,
dangerous indeed,
Sparks of petty jealousy,
On little faults will feed,

He told ye that he loves ye,
Ye ken he'd give his life,
The idea of ye haunts him,
Though ye are my wife

I've always known the strength in you,
Even from the start
I quickly learned to fill the gaps
Now I ken yer heart.

Must I up and kill him then?
Does yer honour need defendin'
Did ye not like his kissing ye,
Was there no a happy endin'

Slapping me will vent yer ire,
He touched without consent,
Is it all out of yer system,
The wave of discontent.

He knows ye neither witch nor whore
For he has married both,
He can nae fathom what ye are,
On that I'll take an oath

## For love of Claire

Forthright in her attitudes,
Immodest in her dress,
She does not care what good folk think,
She intrigues me I confess

At Ardsmuir, he just said she'd gone,
And all supposed her dead,
Yet here she is, large as life,
No Kerch upon her head.

Some call her witch,
She is not that, and I should know I'm sure,
I lived with one who plied that trade,
That knowledge will endure

Healer yes, and clever,
She cannot hide a lie,
Her face will tell her every thought,
And her smile shines through her eye.

She's guilty yes, of many things,
not guilty of this mess,
I stood and watched her brought this low,
A sin I must confess.

I sensed the very truth of it,
My children and their plot,
Hoped they would see reason,
Before she faced the knot

Only I can save her,
I must take the blame,
That would be justice would it not?
In her husband's game.

Maybe we will meet again,
If providence provides,
If we all survive the war,
Although on different sides.

And there she is, no different,
Hair as wild as sin,
Face as open as her mind,
But will she let me in.

To tell her that I love her,
To rashly steal a kiss,
Watch her walk away from me,
As if there's nought amiss,

Is there so much difference
Between that man and I
I would give my life for her,
As he would steal the sky.

James Fraser, man of honour
I envy you your wife,
She's everything I'd ever want,
Guard her with your life,

He does'nae ken ye Sassenach,
He does'nae know yer flaws,
He'd surely die a thousand times,
To know ye don't wear drawers,

When ye get yer dander up
He'd not know to keep clear,
Sure, he's just a Presbyterian
In love with an idea!

# Grand Da's Hill
## Scotland 1980's

The hillside behind Lallybroch,
Amongst the Fraser stones,
With Murray's and Mackenzie's,
Is where he'd lay his bones.

Grand Da says I'll find him here,
He likes it on the hill,
Way up high where he can see
Redcoats coming still.

If ye have tae bury him,
He says this is the spot,
Tis just the place he said he'd be,
We come up here a lot.

He is long dead in our time,
But no grave has been found
Tell me Da are you now
With Ma beneath the ground.

He says he'll always be here,
In everything we do.
Grand Da will look out for Jem,
And for Mandy too!

My kids come here to talk to ghosts,
Is that such a crime?
Or do they speak to Grand Da
Through the years to his own time.

# Tunnel Tiger
## Scotland 1980's

A woman, thrust into their midst,
A woman put in charge,
They'd have their little schoolboy joke,
The jester was at large.

I should have seen it coming,
The sideways, smirking looks,
The plotting and the scheming,
They threaded up their hooks.

The door that led to blackness
Closed and clicked behind.
And one of them has got my torch,
Effectively I'm blind.

I thought of all the options
I cursed them up in heaps,
Now how do I get out of here,
Imagination leaps.

There it was in front of me,
The answer, really plain,
The start of my escape plan
Brianna, take the train.

It hit my like a lightning bolt,
It made my body shake,
Holy god, not here, not now
What's here that makes time quake.

I found the door, I found the light
I found the smirking men.
I swore grave retribution
On the next that calls me 'Hen'

## Aboard the Tranquil Teal
### May 15th, 1777

I watch the coastline disappear,
Quill in hand, I think
What tae write and tell ye,
Without wasting precious ink.

We are aboard the Tranquil Teal,
A doughty smugglers ketch,
Trustworthy is the captains name,
Excuse me while I retch!

Me, yer Ma, and Ian
Din'nae forget the dog
Headed to Connecticut
On this god forsaken log.

We travel light, all we have
It hidden in our coats,
The biggest thing I carry
Is ma strong hatred of boats.

Ma hand won't let me write much more,
Neither will yer ma,
Suffice to say we are in good health,
Your ever loving – Da

And here is the news
May 15th, 1777


There's more tae write, of Fergus,
Ken yer mother has the quill,
Quite a strammash in New Bern
But he has nae come off ill.

Whilst out on his paper rounds,
A sack put o'er his head,
They dragged him from his mule cart,
But would nae have him dead.

He fought them off with gusto,
Before his goose could cook,
They ran off when he drew their blood,
But someone stole his hook.

The loyalists deny it,
They say he prints for them,
The rebels didn't do it
He's for freedom don't ye ken.

Why would they deport him,
And put him in a sack,
Why would they tar and feather him,
They know he'd fight them back.

Then there is Percy Beauchamp,
His ear to the ground,
He's thorough in his homework,
The history he'll have found.

I fear that Fergus Fraser
Juggled too many balls,
And with only one hand and a hook
He's heading for the falls.

But Fergus is a Frenchman
With Scottish wits for bye,
He'll keep on dodging capture
And print sedition on the sly!

## Post Script

Letter fit fer posting,
Yer Ma has writ a lot,
Her hand is stronger yet that mine,
There's nought she has forgot

I see I have the last word,
These days the chance I rare
There's things I have tae tell ye,
Treat them with great care!

If ought should now befall us,
Or if we just get old,
There's goods that the Italian left,
That history enfolds

He does nae know what lies there
I'd not leave so much trace
Tell him tae find the Spaniard,
Young Jemmy knows this place.

I ken the house has found ye,
Sometimes I can see
Your faces in my old man's dreams
Please kiss the weans for me.

I must go, I've had my word
Ken, women run this place
There's eight of them when counted last,
And yer Ma is on my case

Your loving father
JF

## Beware of Cameron

Rob Cameron – hand of friendship
Rob Cameron – letter thief
Rob Cameron – kidnaps children
He is warped beyond belief.

Cameron's are avaricious
And Cameron's are sly
Cameron's manipulate
Cameron's will lie.

There was danger in that letter,
I felt it in the pen,
No one else would know the cave,
It would be lost again.

What is the connection,
Is he Hectors kin,
He tries to come back to the past,
He seeks the gold ye ken.

Jem and Mandy hear me,
They can reach me through the veil
They will lead ye back to me,
Guide ye down the trail.

I din'nae dream of everything,
I sense things are awry,
Beware of Cameron he seeks the gold
He will nae let it lie.

## With Intent
### Scotland 1980's

Armed with steel and diamonds
I left them at the stones,
Could they bring our Jemmy back,
Would travel crush their bones,

In the darkness of the study,
Of history I read,
In letters from my fathers,
Took note of what each said.

Both sought to protect me,
Both had not been wrong,
How greed for gold corrodes a mind
And how I must stay strong.

I hear footsteps in the hall,
Do I detect a ghost,
A man treads heavy on the boards,
To whom do I play host.

You! What business have you here,
And where's my bloody son,
Get him back, you bastard,
With you I am not done.

Hen! it's you I've come for,
And he'll tell me to ma face,
Of the Spaniard in the letter,
And the hiding place.

He's safe, but ye'll not find him,
Yer husband mind, he's lost.
I'm in charge you'll do my will,
Now get yer clothes off Boss.

Time ye had a shafting,
Same as I have lass,
Let's see how ye like it hen
Tae take it up the arse.

Jeans removed I swung them,
Wrapped around his head,
Use the sword from off the wall
Or the cricket bat instead.

Cameron left unconscious,
He has to be alive,
He knows where Jem is hidden,
He must at least survive.

I put him in the Priest hole
That way he'll not go far,
I hope there's ghosts there with him
And he's sharing it with Da!

## The Priest Hole

'Tween the cellar and the kitchen,
Underneath the floor,
Space to hide a person,
When safety is unsure,

Built to hide a fugitive,
It never hid a priest,
In days when Redcoats raided,
Some sanctuary at least.

The ghost of the Dunbonnet
The ghosts of wanted men
He'll be there in the company,
Of highland ghosts ye ken.

Cameron can sit there,
And contemplate escape,
Maybe Da will visit,
And teach him not tae rape.

## Dear Deadeye,
### Scotland 1980's

If and when you read this,
It may well be old news,
Your mother may have told you,
For it was hers to choose.

Though you call me father,
You do not have my genes,
Your sire is a highland Scot,
All is not how it seems.

I know she will go back to him
I felt his pull for years,
I could not salve her heartache,
I could not dry the tears.

The record of her marriage
Recorded in his time,
Fraser marries Beauchamp
She didn't marry him with mine!

I still don't quite believe it,
But research shows it true,
I know that you may follow her,
And some may follow you.

I hope I have prepared you well,
I started in your youth
You've always been my special girl
I swear that is the truth.

Be aware of prophecies,
And those that hold belief,
Who seek to find a Scottish heir
Born of a Highland chief

Now go and find your destiny,
In whatever year
I know whose girl you really are,
Do it without fear

Take the book and read it well,
Tell him he's me to thank
I shall always be here watching you
Your loving father Frank.

## Whore of Babylon

Her brethren are all safe inside,
Shut up in the coop,
She sits and waits upon her perch,
Left out of the loop,

Why would one choose this lofty branch
To sit out in the rain,
To not avoid the coming storm
The answer should be plain

Tis not a conscious effort
She has not that much sense
She'll not submit to prison
Surrounded by a fence.

Tis nothing like a conscious thought
For chickens have no wits,
Tis just a bid for freedom
And that's the end of it.

He calls her whore of Babylon,
This bird who is perverse,
When wind picks up and rain comes in,
I've called her far far worse.

All is sold, for we must leave,
New furrows we must plough
A chicken hiding up a tree
Is not my problem now.

## To bite the hand

Meeting is community,
Tis more than weekly prayer,
Brethren will look after you
When others may not care,

Meeting found some relative,
Far across the sea,
A calling there for Denny,
And loneliness for me

They taught me all a woman needs,
They prayed and took us in,
Brought us up to live a life
Quite devoid of sin.

Now Denny is a doctor,
An educated man,
He speaks his mind, says what he feels
Not always the best plan.

Philadelphia meeting prayed,
They are against a war,
Do not disturb the status quo,
He had heard it all before.

The spirit moved my brother,
For freedom he would speak,
We must stand for liberty
Protection of the weak.

He stood for independence,
Freedom from the Crown,
That would not come without a fight,
on violence Quakers frown.

We'd bit the hand that fed us,
Decided, without doubt,
The Philadelphia Elders met,
The Hunters were 'Put Out'

Pariahs now, we have no place
All will turn their backs
I go with my brother
On an independent track

## Before the Siege

Notches on a doorpost,
Counting down the days,
How many days' til freedom,
I slackened off my stays,

Deep in contemplation,
He paced around the ground,
The Colonel of militia,
Hangdog as a hound.

The British are a coming,
And they come in force,
Ticonderoga will be took,
We know this now, of course.

I fell in step beside him,
Felt the fire in his blood,
St Clair didn't listen then?,
Well, I did'na think he would.

Let's walk in the garden,
I produced the only key,
Extracted from the kitchen hand
When no one else could see.

He watched me then intently,
Undressed me with his eyes,
Sassenach I need yer help,
I admit to some surprise.

I teased him to distraction,
Did what he had asked
Falling in the long grass,
Intent no longer masked

Tell me what you're thinking,
He whispered in my ear,
His spare hand clamped upon my mouth,
Lest passers-by should hear

Pinned down underneath him,
I heard his hidden thought,
Revenge was swift and oh so sweet
My inner muscles taught.

He'd been a virgin, not a monk
He does not often ask for help
Then I can make him call his Lord,
And he will hear me yelp.

## Bemis Heights

On me boys, at the gallop,
Protect the Brigadier,
Rebel snipers fill the trees,
He has no sense of fear.

On me lads, there's no turning
Steady! hold the line,
We gathered to our leader,
Dodged the bullets whine.

A target by his uniform
He took one in the side
Hanging gut shot from his horse,
Far too weak to ride.

I saw the barrel gleaming,
I heard the rifle crack.
Felt my tricorn leave my head,
I wouldn't get that back.

Damn the Rebel whoreson,
If his aim was true
My brains would be at Bemis Heights,
God damn you man in blue

A tongue not heard since childhood
Speaks quiet in the dark.
Comfort for a dying man,
The Rebel leaves his mark.

Imposing man, commands respect
He comes here to his kin,
A final word, a last farewell
Both leaders to their skin.

The quacks have tried their hardest
The priest has said his part
The Rebel General sits and talks
Deaths journey must now start.

And as we walked back to the lines,
He handed me his hat,
Still warm from wear, and has no nits,
A perfect fit at that.

I knew the man, I knew the voice
I knew this was not luck
Twice he's fired and twice he's missed.
Next time I'd better duck!

1st November 1777, New York

## Wall Street

I write to you from New York,
And we are all alive,
Battle worn and weary,
I'm sure we will survive.

I've had to mend your father,
He's been under the knife,
His crippled finger is now gone,
at least he kept his life.

We travel with a kinsman,
Our job to take him home,
See him safe to Scotland,
Across the oceans foam.

It will be hard to lose him,
His cabin lined with lead,
Is a very heavy coffin,
Simon Fraser is quite dead.

We take him home to Balnain,
To rest in Scottish loam,
Then destination Lallybroch
Taking Ian home.

Your father writes a post script,
He's testing out his hand,
He will not let me watch him,
In case it doesn't go as planned.
*

Dear Daughter, I have seen him safe,
He will not fight in this war,
Your brother goes to England,
The surrender made that sure.

Ye ken I've lost a finger,
Yer mother told ye how,
Her surgery is a bonnie job,
I'm a better pen man now,

I'm signing off on all saints feast,
Please say one for my soul,
Ye ken how much I hate the sea,
A prayer might keep me whole!

Your loving father
JF

20th December 1777

## Edinburgh Spectacular

There's a woman looking at me,
She's dressed in brown and gold,
I think she's seen a lot of life,
But doesn't look that old,

Her hair is shot with silver,
It curls around her face,
Her skin is clear, her eyes are bright
Of war there's little trace.

The winter bitten hungered look
Of living on ones wits
Hasn't yet invaded her,
Or any of her bits,

Not dressed like a pauper,
Not suffering from lack
HM's Navy fed us well,
On the voyage back.

They suit ye lass, I hear him say
They're bonnie on yer face,
Accept ye needed spectacles,
I take this with good grace.

Sassenach ye wear it well,
After all the times we've had,
A little tweaking here and there,
Ye din'nae scrub up bad.

Remorseless Scott, be quiet
Must you lower the tone,
I'm starting to enjoy the view,
Through these lenses of my own.

Looking in the mirror,
I haven't done in years,
I see him there behind me,
And I'd love to box his ears,

He sees me now through steel rimmed frames,
With rose tint in the glass,
He may be looking at my face,
His hands are on my arse.

Sassenach you look beautiful,
Yer eyes now rimmed with gold,
Ladylike, distinguished,
And not any less bold!

I am no longer eagle eyed,
But even I can see
Yer beauty leap through every pore,
And ye've only eyes fer me.

Let's away tae Mowbray's,
Ye'll be needing a good feed,
Ye have nae met wee Andy Bell,
He's a spectacle indeed.

# A Bonnie, Concubine

He does nae rise til lunchtime,
He parties until dawn,
Wee Andy Bell will sleep away
The hours of the morn.

A man who uses ladders
To climb down from his horse,
The horse is either very tall,
Or the man is short of course!

Arrival with a flourish,
And ceremony due,
Andy Bell, come join us man,
Come and take a pew!

As short as tall men sitting down,
A conformation mess,
A twisted spine and big hooked nose,
But fashionable dress.

A formidable character,
Well known in the town,
He jokes of his appearance,
Barely wears a frown.

Etcher and engraver,
He's not getting a pass,
This man has taken liberties
With Jamie's Bonnie lass.

He tries to pay with whisky,
And tales of Bon Viveur
There's only one thing Jamie wants,
Money is the cure.

Twelve years rent was needless
He used her from the start,
Andy Bell will pay his due,
For the Bonnie printed art.

## Pressing Business

Let's get down tae business
Let's cut tae the chase,
Twill take much more than whisky
Put a smile upon ma face,

Andy Bell looked sheepish,
Ye'll have called at the shop?
Well, her work has so much beauty man
It seemed a shame tae stop.

Has ma Bonnie been yer concubine
Fer all of twelve long years?
And I've been paying lodge fer her,
Yer driving me tae tears.

Well, I've used but no' abused her,
Ye'll find her good as new,
I'm sure there's common ground here,
The deal is there tae do.

Cut to the hotel cellar,
A stench to raise the dead,
General Frasers rotting corpse
Is leaking through the lead

Wee Andy helped to the rescue,
With maggots and with bran,
The bones will get to Balnain,
With all the speed we can.

A deal was done for printing,
I mean to write a book,
I've negotiated copies
But I knew you'd want a look.

Cheeky little skinflint,
Ye'll have it leather bound,
And copies for the colonies,
So, a compromise was found.

Also in the package,
Himself would get to pen,
Stories writ by Grand Da,
On for the weans ken!

I scratched my head and dipped my quill
Just where would I start,
A French fop downstairs for ye ma'am
Disturbs the writer's art!

Why would Percy Beauchamp
Come calling at my door,
No good can come for Fergus
From what he knows, I'm sure.

Politics and intrigue,
Quite beyond the pale,
With Fergus in the middle,
And a country up for sale.

## Ode to Bonnie

She understands my every word,
Is silent unless told,
Only speaks when spoken to,
And then in typeface bold,

A lady with a subtle tongue,
In language she's adept,
Guided by her masters hand,
Around the law she stepped,

A body formed of iron cast,
A heart of hardened steel
A soul baptised in font of lead,
Free, she will nae kneel.

I'd sheath my dirk, lay down my gun
And take her by the hand,
This canny lass will speak my mind
And broadcast to the land.

I will take her 'cross the sea,
Fair maid who does my will,
Mightier than any sword
To those who'd read their fill,

My Bonnie lass, we'll have some fun
Speak what every man desires
Spread the words of freedom,
Dance between life's fires.

When I was lost she was ma voice,
Her words would tell my life,
Obedient in every way,
Much more so than ma wife

## A Big Mistake

My old room, from a wee small boy,
A day remembered well,
My wedding day to Laoghaire
The match was made in hell.

Reflection in the water,
My face and thoughts askew,
With each scrape of the razor,
A stranger came to view

A new shirt sewn together,
From all that we could find,
The preacher waiting patient,
Panic in my mind.

To be part of a family,
To find myself a place,
Find some happiness and peace,
The past try to erase.

I'd felt a stirring in ma kilt,
That's one worry eased,
At the thought of bedding,
Ma cock at least was pleased.

Second thoughts were banished,
I could nae let them down,
So, Ian walked me to my fate,
And vows made with a frown.

Twas wrong of me to do it,
I could nae give her love,
Ma mind was never with her,
It was with you my dove.

She did'na want my pity,
She thought she held my heart,
Or at least I needed her,
Mistaken from the start,

Days of tears and silence,
One long domestic frost,
No laughter on the menu,
No zest in life the cost.

Marsali and Joannie
My only joy in life
I was the Da they never had
But I did'na need a wife

Laoghaire Mackenzie,
How many years must pass,
I was married to a woman,
You will always be a lass!

Your fetch was at the altar Claire,
Your ghost lay in our bed,
Twas only you could heal me,
She could only wish ye dead.

# The Grief of Parting
## 20th April 1778

I think tae weep ye need tae feel
All I feel is numb,
I sit here looking at the door,
I wait fer ye tae come,

I ken that now ye have nae pain
Yer in a better place,
Still, I sit and look fer you,
I can'nae see yer face.

Yer chair is ever empty,
Ma bed tis halfways cold,
I never thought tae be like this,
And not sae very old.

Ye bore it all wi patience,
Wi humour dry as bone,
While coughing tore yer lungs apart,
And dried ye up like stone.

The lord says that I must forgive,
I can'nae do that yet,
And the cruelty of the English,
I never shall forget.

No longer is this place ma home,
'Tis time for me tae leave,
I shall go wi ma brother then,
Will ye tell me not tae grieve,

Jamie says ye are with him
Always to his right,
So, on my other side ye'll lie.
When I sleep at night.

I have nae wept, I can'nae feel
I think tis called bereft,
My heart is empty as a shell,
Whose owner up and left

Ian if yer listening,
I ken I talk tae much,
I shall always have ye wi' me,
And hunger for yer touch.

Yer Will is read, all debts are paid,
All things handed on,
My bags are packed, ma brother waits
'Tis time that I was gone.

Before I rise, there's just one thing,
'Tis preying on ma mind,
If yer body lies in Scotland
Should I leave yer leg behind!

# Asthma Attack

Headquarters of the British,
I go to tell my tale,
Lord John? – I don't know where he is
I've searched without avail.

Recalled to the army,
Commission all renewed
Panic starts to grow inside,
It will not be subdued.

A man stands in the corner,
A cloud of golden lace,
Lord Johns stamp but older,
This must be 'His Grace'

Yes, my name is Harold
And yes I am a Duke,
Pardloe is the title,
My god I think I'll puke.

Welcome to the family,
With charm, my words he parried,
My dear, you must call me Hal,
I'd no idea he'd married.

Yes, he'd called on Henry,
Of course, that is his son!
And Dottie too and William,
The family visits done.

He is not here for pleasure,
His army lines the shore,
The duke seeks out his Officers
He's here to fight a war.

Pray now, where's my brother,
He asks me, nice as pie,
Believe I see straight through your face,
I will know it if you lie!

Escorted home, the truth may out,
Hal will have to wait,
Lord John is gone I know not where,
In Jamie's hands his fate.

Germaine to the rescue
The rabble are dispersed,
No one shall harm his Grannie,
For they will come off worst

The hand of fate, or providence
The duke is robbed of breath
Asthma, a severe attack
It could lead to his death.

Breathe in two three, And out to three
Breathe long without objection,
Just concentrate on breathing
You are under my protection

Confined to bed and in my care,
This solution is quite neat,
Hal is now our prisoner
In the house on Chestnut Street.

## No Bed Involved

He says ye went tae bed wi' him,
My insides quite dissolved,
No! I said succinctly,
There was no 'bed' involved.

It started on the furniture,
It ended on the floor,
cathartic and violent,
No love involved, I'm sure,

For days I'd sat and grieved for you,
Pondered my own death,
Listed ways to end my life,
Not take one more breath,

He would have no more of it,
We both had lost a love,
One he was not entitled to,
As mine was, hand and glove,

There was a lot of brandy drunk,
With not a lot of care,
Both of us were joined in flesh
To a man who was not there,

That night we bared our mortal souls,
With you we both lay,
He with you, I not with him,
He's not my sort I'd say!

His arms were yours around me,
Your death left me forlorn,
He applied a carnal salve
Which shattered with the dawn.

And now you stand before me,
Demanding, with some gall,
I thought you dead my soul was lost,
John Grey saved me, that's all!

## Meeting as Friends

Uniforms and Highland dress,
Meet this time as friends,
Two families, both torn by war,
Hostilities suspend.

Two couples joined together,
In love as clear as glass,
The physician and the Duchess,
The Mohawk and his lass,

We walked along the river,
Talked as couples do,
The lassies will be sore, the morn!
Well, the men may be that too!

Denny, is a surgeon,
ye ken he'll have a book,
When Dottie asked me for advice,
I told her where to look,

What did ye tell her Sassenach,
I ken ye have yer whiles!
Ye did'na tell her that one!
Well, that should make him smile

And Rachel too, ye told her that
Won't Ian think it odd,
His Quaker lass, his virgin bride,
Will make him call for God,

We fell to reminiscing,
Our highland wedding night,
Not a monk he'd told me,
He didn't ken I'd bite!

He talked of natural talent,
Things I'd taught him well,
Of waking bruised and sated,
And still under my spell,

Let's go home then Sassenach,
His tongue ran up my neck,
He lit the flame inside me,
One not to keep in check,

Make me call his name out loud,
And I'll see what I can do,
I've a few tricks still up ma kilt
Tae get a squeak from you.

Ye make me say 'oh god' each day,
With things ye've done or said,
Most of them tae do with life,
And nought tae do wi' bed.

## Stinking Papist

Is it fate which ties us,
Our paths seem linked and crossed,
He turns up, unexpectedly,
Every time I'm lost!

Cousin, did he call me?
Now I see it's sense,
Scottish, bloody Mohawk,
His painted gaze intense.

My mind cannot make sense of this,
It whirls around my brain,
Every time I think of it
It only causes pain,

Am I a stinking papist,
Did Mac give me that name,
He and General Fraser,
Are they one and the same

Uncle Hal respects him,
Papa is his great friend,
That Scottish Mohawk is his kin,
On whom can I depend?!

He that shot my hat off,
It might have been my head,
He that spoke in Gaelic
At my Brigadiers bed.

Those wooden beads I threw at him,
I miss them round my neck,
In times of pain and trouble
My hand goes there to check,

To cast aside my heritage,
To put aside my life,
Accept my sire is who he is,
And she not Papa's wife.

Mother Claire, is Mother Claire,
Whichever path I choose,
And she's a constant they both love,
And one I would not loose!

The question he won't answer,
Will remain unsaid,
I'll never know exactly why,
He took mama to bed.

He calls her brave, not flighty,
Headstrong, not a whore,
He takes her blame upon himself,
A penance he'd endure,

Regretful of her passing,
Shameful of her death,
But not sorry for my birth,
I hear under his breath.

# I Spy

Blended in the background,
The ever-present ear,
The eye that sees into a life,
And casts a shaft of fear,

Hiding in the shadows,
Seeking out their prey,
Every army has its spies,
Faceless men in grey,

You would not give them notice,
Standing in a room,
Chameleons of intrigue,
Blending with the gloom,

Plausible and eloquent,
Hiding in plain sight,
What colour then his coat today,
What side of the fight.

Richardson the grey man,
Has changed from Red to Blue,
From loyalist to rebel,
But is this really true.

Keep yer wits about ye,
Yer wee knife at yer side,
Already he's played games wi' you,
Made you Lord Johns bride.

Sassenach he'll come again,
He'll try and play ye false
God knows what and God knows how,
Din'nae join his waltz.

He found me in my surgery,
Devious, shifty man,
Cards upon the table time,
The spy outlined his plan.

He sought me as an agent,
But Jamie spoiled his game,
No longer family to Hal,
He'd use me just the same.

Pardloe lobbies London
Seeking terms for peace,
Richardson is all for war,
The fight then must not cease,

He seeks a source of blackmail
A tool to stop the duke,
Would I give him Lord John Grey,
The thought near made me puke.

Leave this place and leave it now,
I've a patient to attend,
You will not get your dirt from me,
I don't mean to offend!

Ezekiel Richardson,
Hastened from my door
Time and tide determine
If our paths should cross once more.

## Sophronia

Brought here by her mistress,
A woman in despair,
Taken to her masters bed,
Damaged beyond repair.

Her baby cut inside her,
Her insides torn apart,
I could mend the physical,
I cannot mend her heart!

He wept, she told me he was sad,
The master of her life,
Her child lost had made him cry,
Not so, his callous wife.

Ether, breath it deeply child,
You shall not feel the pain,
My sutures will seal up the wounds,
Make you whole again.

All sewn up, fistulae gone,
All connected right,
Should I take one extra step,
Prevent another mite.

It is her life, you saw her grief
Do not play God today
Thee can't decide her future
Don't take her choice away,

Rachel speaks compassion,
It's not my call to make,
Even when the outcome
Is another man's mistake.

Her master will still take her,
Tis not ours to decide,
She is his slave, his property,
He will not be denied

Desperation on her voice
Muffled by her hand,
I tried my best, 'twas not my fault
It wasn't what god planned

# A meet with evil

Reflected by the darkness
Reflection of insight,
Reflex action, tunes his mind
Reaction for this night,

Focussed on infinity
Focussed on the past,
Time once more to call the roll,
To find out who stands fast

Eyes that see me watching,
But are not seeing back,
Connected now with other times,
Preparing for attack.

A change of clothes, A warriors garb,
His armour worn with pride,
Discarded once upon the moor,
Where once a country died,

Voices cry in darkness,
It's them I hear ye ken,
The battle yell, before the charge,
The cries of highland men.

Dressed with care to meet them,
To roll the dice of life,
Deal the cards, play his hand,
Then come home to his wife.

din'nae fash now Sassenach,
He does'nae want me dead,
He needs me for a trophy,
Hold that thought in yer head,

It will nae be sae pleasant,
I would nae give ye fright,
The captain means tae force ma hand,
There's evil in this night.

# Men who talk in corners

Ritual and business,
The order of the night,
Formality, normality,
Conversation, light.

Tight lipped was the greeting,
Thoughts writ upon his face,
The matters of the evening
Conducted with good grace,

Minor spats and quarrels
Disputes solved tween the men,
Gossip which could lead to strife
Adjudicated then.

Men who talk in corners,
But loud, just to be heard,
Talk of loyalty to Crown,
I hear their every word,

Is this it then, the trigger,
What answers would he know
I've some prepared, but none sae great
As those from long ago,

As long as there's a hundred,
As my forefathers believe,
Time to quote the great Arbroath.
And then tis time tae leave.

Melt into the darkness,
A stealthy highland fox,
Vanish deep into the night,
With dirk and pistol cocked!

# Pest Control

Dear Mrs Fraser

A letter short and to the point,
A line or two at best,
Pardloe doesn't waste a word
To get things off his chest.

He has a rodent problem,
He doesn't mean a mouse,
A rat threatens the honour
Of his ancient loyal house

Can I suggest a poison,
To rid him of this plague,
I could make a few suggestions
But best I keep things vague.

He's going on a journey
A dangerous sojourn
I'm to look after his brother
Should he not return.

Signed off with no flourish
No best regards et al
He just comes swiftly to the end
And signs off H for Hal!

# Perseverance

A man of little substance,
A coward to the core,
A lack of moral fibre,
How I loved this man before

Handsome yes, and charming
Filled with social grace,
This butterfly, this Francophile
How dare he show his face.

Is yellow skin worth saving,
He's hung me out to dry,
Our darkest secrets all revealed,
Oh, Perseverance why?

You'd see me on the gallows,
For Richardson won't crack,
And Hal is likely out of town
Never to come back.

Perseverance Wainwright
One thing I ask of you,
Take my son a message,
He will know what to do.

Sorry doesn't cut it,
Tears will do no good,
The man who holds me hostage,
Is a man of devious blood.

Once I called you brother,
I thought of you as kin,
I lay with you as lover
Committed mortal sin.

Go then Perseverance,
Tail between your legs,
I know that you will save yourself,
Do what the devil begs.

Dearest Perseverance
Did you find it hard,
To tell him all and save your skin,
And hang mine from the yard

# Digitalis

Dear Hal

As regards a poison,
I could recommend a few
A brew made out of foxgloves
Should do the job for you.

Steep in boiling water,
Brew for minutes three
Some cake and bread and butter,
You can serve your rat high tea

If tea is not your cuppa
This one is a winner
Serve the leaves as salad
And invite them round for dinner!

Advice on digitalis,
Please keep under your hat
Tis not a pleasant way to die
Even for a rat.

I signed it off Claire Fraser
I blotted dry the ink
What is Pardloe up to
I didn't like to think,

What are ye thinking Sassenach,
He read it upside down,
He looked at me with eyebrows raised,
And half a Scottish frown.

I ken ye speak with tongue in cheek,
With all that ye suggest
But when it comes tae pest control
Pardloe does'nae jest!

## Black Brandy

Black Brandy, Blood of Martyrs
Red, Amber in the light
The bottle under lock and key
The smell and taste not right.

All is consternation
As Percy gabbles on
No comfort in his message,
Great danger here for John.

Bolstered up with liquor,
His tale of woe was told,
The ship will sail, upon the tide,
We need an action bold,

Adjourning to the garden,
Private words exchange
What to do, where to go,
With what is John arraigned

In a house with secrets
Best not help yourself
What Hal put in that bottle
Is not good for the health

Percy lies upon the floor,
His eyes an empty space,
Black the Brandy bottle,
His heartbeat just a trace,

There is no way to save his life,
The foxglove did its job
That much digitalis
The life from man will rob.

Oh William, you did your best
His heart came to a halt,
This overdose is fatal,
It can't be cured with salt

## My Father's House

I rode for days through hard terrain,
Slept rough upon the ground,
In my mind I wrote my speech
But few words could be found.

Dripping rain on canvas,
Listening to the trees,
The forest never seems to sleep
I'm exhausted to my knees.

One eye always open
That eye too tired for sight,
Bears pad past on silent feet,
And I too tired for fright!

A Horse pressed to her limits,
A Man pressed way past fear,
Where would I find my journeys end
That winding path not clear

Then there it was in front of me
Glinting in the sun,
A house, a home of substance
With people, overrun.

Welcomed there with open arms,
Help offered without terms
Food and drink, and then a bed,
And this not squashing worms.

Belly full to bursting,
Covers keep me warm,
I know that with my father's help,
We will face the coming storm.

# Healing Hands

Night is when the body heals
When bone and flesh restore,
When old wounds stretch, and new ones knit
The sleeper wakes up sore,

This morning finds my patient,
Sitting on the bed,
Half asleep, irascible
Hands resting on his head

A restless night of twitching
As old scars stretched their length
As new ones flexed and mended
Then tested their own strength,

Ageing doesn't come alone
What does come as a shock,
Is waking to the feeling
Someone's standing on yer cock

What are ye up to Sassenach?
I've warm tea in my mouth,
Hand checking his anatomy
I start my journey south

din'nae take it literal,
Twas just a metaphor
Sassenach ma balls are fine,
They din'nae need a cure

I can sense ye laughing,
I feel oblivions pull,
Did no one ever tell ye
din'nae talk with yer mouth full

I'd best lie back, enjoy the trip
Matters are in hand
I'll just mutter words in Gaelic
That she can nae understand

# The third level

Purgatory has levels,
For the cleansing of the soul
Admission into heaven
This is the final goal,

The book of Jeremiah speaks
this is what he'd say,
One way to heaven, one to hell,
Is this another way?

Through muttered Gaelic cursing,
I hear him push through pain,
That knee must be made stronger,
If he wants to walk again.

The therapy of exercise,
To bend and stretch the joint,
Painful now, and like a man
He cannot see the point.

Jamie would you spend your life
Walking with a stick,
If not, do your lunges
And do them double quick!

Ye have me at yer mercy,
Yet torture me my love
How can ye bear to watch my pain,
My Angel from above.

Have ye no mortal kindness,
Slave driver of my heart
Sassenach ye are a witch,
Ye were one from the start,

Ye can'nae bribe me Sassenach
With honey on ma bread,
Or the gossip from the kitchen
With which ye fill yer head

When it's time for press ups,
I shall have revenge for sure,
I shall pin ye underneath me,
Ye can shield me from the floor!

# Lists

Lists of things that go with us,
Lists of things to stay,
Lists of people listing jobs,
Lists of roles to play.

Planning who will need to come,
Who needs to remain,
In charge in our absence,
The Mackenzie's I explain.

He and I are easy,
We've often gone to war,
Our belongings up and pack themselves,
As they have done before.

Harder then, to organise
The running of the Ridge,
And watch two Frasers prowling,
Trying to build a bridge.

This time we go for Williams sake,
Hunting for Lord John,
A chance to reconciliate?
More of that anon.

# Garden of life

Fertile earth I feel it's pull
Wrapped around my fingers,
All of life is started here,
And at the end, here lingers.

Soil and sun and water,
A never-ending ring,
Shoots will grow and flourish,
In the trees the birds will sing,

We do not own the flowers,
We do not own the trees,
We harness all earths bounty,
We borrow from the bees.

The colours of the wilderness
Tamed here by my hand
Here is where I order thoughts
He may not understand.

Here he cannot read a mind,
Where hopes grow like the grass,
Where fears are hidden in the weeds,
Behind a face of glass

Where life renews in seasons,
Where nature builds its bridge,
Regrets, I tell them to the bees,
In my garden on the ridge.

He watches from the gateway,
He sees my cares release,
Knows I'm in my happy place
My little patch of peace,

## Fear Returns

I ken yer scairt, SHE shows it,
Tis plain upon Claire's face,
You hide yer inner feelings,
On you I see no trace.

Tis her lives with ma dreaming,
Who knows when in they creep
Kens the ghosts that haunt me
That taunt me in ma sleep

I fear the most for William
As father fears for son,
For him this is adventure aye,
For one sae bold, and young.

I ken the depths a man can reach
When cruelty fills a mind
What depths of degradation
The torturer may find.

John has nae been a captive,
Since he was but a whelp,
I fear what they may do to him,
I fear I can'nae help

I've welcome ghosts that call on me,
Those that are my kin,
Then there are those of men I've killed,
In war or mortal sin.

I've owned ma' ghosts fer half a life,
Claire has seen them all,
The ones which make me sweat and scream
The ones which make me crawl.

From her I have no secrets,
In sleep she hears the truth
The strange nocturnal visitors
Who have been there since my youth.

When I wake, the ghosts are gone
And I must face the day,
I don again the Fraser mask
And hide the fears away.

She knows which ones are welcome
Which ones will cause me fright
Her face displays my greatest fear,
Jack Randall came last night.

## Two Hundred Days

Gods waiting room is crowded,
All shall have their turn,
Forgiveness and their seat with him,
Or some will rightly burn,

Each will have their time to bide,
But none will see the queue,
Reflection and the time tae think,
To ponder, like ye do,

The things that ye regret in life
The things yer glad ye did,
The things yer proud tae shout about,
The things Ye'd best keep hid.

All are here, recorded,
They gave meaning tae yer life,
But always there's a price tae pay,
In this waiting room of strife.

I must sit two hundred years,
Then, with penance done,
I may walk the halls again,
Tae find ma chosen one.

I see ye read the pages,
And ye din'nae ken the end,
I am waiting with ye,
Yer ever patient friend,

Ye dissect every sentence,
In yer quest to find the truth,
The truth is known to but a few,
And written in my youth.

Will ye pick my life apart,
I thought that Gods own role,
Or that of she who holds the quill
To write my final goal.

Can ye no be patient,
Two hundred years I'll pause
Ye've only had two hundred days,
To list ma many flaws.

I see ye raise an eyebrow,
We're ye expecting rain,
Or just looking to the Lord above,
To quench the drought again

## Acknowledgements

As always, my first acknowledgement is to the written word of Diana Gabaldon wo has been the inspiration for all these poems and rhymes. Acknowledgment also to the makers of the Outlander Series.
To Lynn Fuller the immensely talented lady who allows me to use her work on my covers and also creates new versions of her work for my use

# Copyright

Other Books by the Author
The Author has also written a series of books of
poetry based on the Outlander Television
Series:

Unofficial Droughtlander Relief.

The Droughtlander's Progress.

Totally Obsessed.

Fireside Stories.

Je Suis Prest.

Après Le Deluge

Dragonflies of Summer

Semper in Aeternum

Sia air Ochd

Intervallaqua

Facing the Storm

The Blue Vase

Mille Basia Volume 1

Mille Basia Vol 2

These are also sold to raise money for RDA – If you are a fan of the series try them, they have received some excellent reviews from purchasers.

I hope the Princess will Approve – a book of COVID and Horse related poems.

· · · · · · · · · · · · · · · · · · · · · · · · · · · · · · · · · · · · · · · · · · · · ·

Ginger like Biscuits - the adventures of a Welsh Mountain Pony. – a short book written for young teenaged horse enthusiasts.

A recipe for disaster - poems about the authors life.

All are published through Amazon

Or sold through the authors Etsy Shop poemsandthings


Email: chestyathome@aol.com

# The End

Printed in Great Britain
by Amazon

22085552R00088